AF350401

The Nazi's Daughter

Also by Judy Shuler

Red & Blue: A Memoir of Two Alaskan Tour Guides (with Hildegard Ratliff)
Safe Harbor: Stories of Enduring Friendship
You Too Can Haiku: Journaling in Three Lines

The Nazi's Daughter

Judy Shuler

Ouzel Press

Fredonia, NY

Copyright© 2026 Judy Shuler

ISBN 979-8-218-84804-0

This is a work of fiction inspired by lived experiences of the children of World War II. Names, characters, places, and events are either products of the author's imagination or are used in a made-up way.

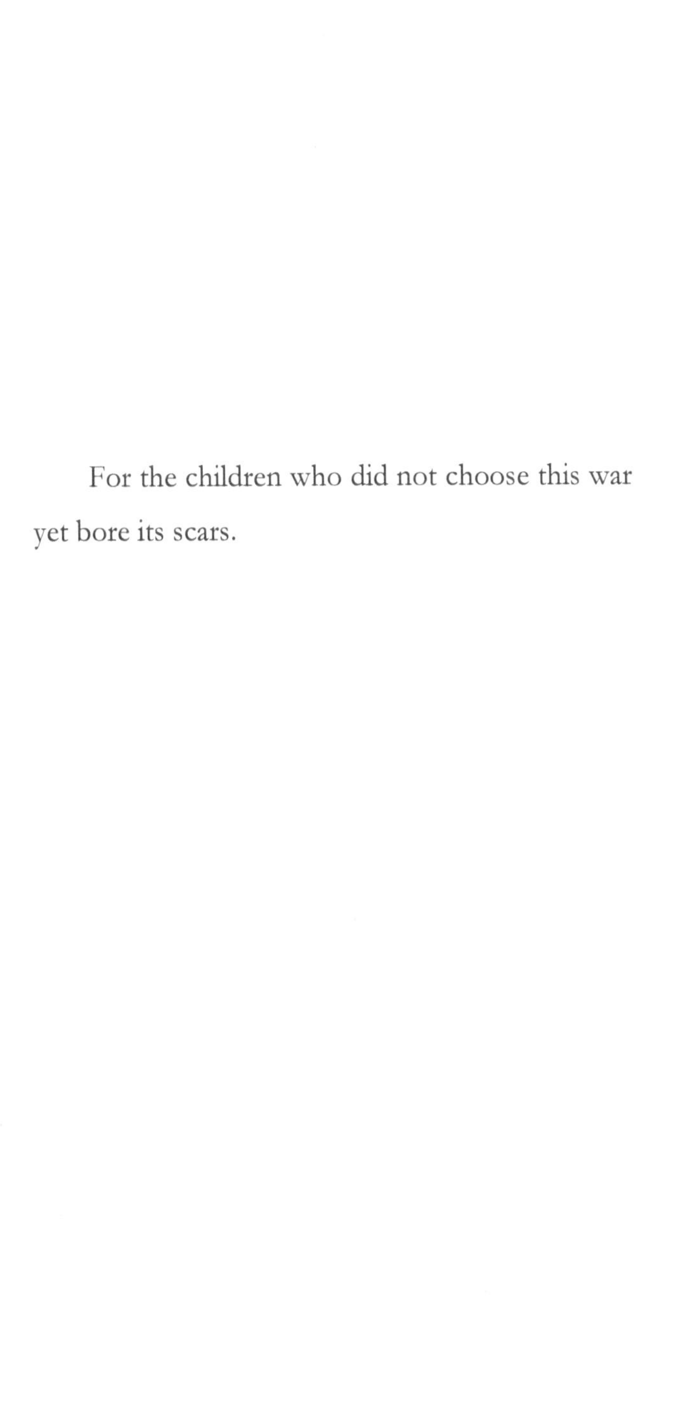

For the children who did not choose this war
yet bore its scars.

Acknowledgments

Thanks to members of Write Focus Writers' Group at Ahira Hall Library, Brocton, NY, for their ongoing support; to Lakeshore Center for the Arts, Westfield, NY, for giving Gisela a new voice; and to Barbara Bilicki for her comprehensive and thoughtful editing.

1

THE RECLINER

Gisela opens blinds to an early spring day on the High Plains. The sliding glass doors face east, the rising sun still low enough in the sky to stream deep into her condominium, through her living room and into a compact kitchen. She scans daffodil shoots just beyond the screened-in lanai, looking for signs of buds that usher in her favorite and most hopeful time of year.

When it warms, she will hang an American flag on a bracket outside.

There are regulations about what can be hung outside, but flags are allowed and even encouraged, and she says flags just make you feel good.

Gisela lives a life alone now, much of it in a gray recliner.

A command center of sorts, the chair is where she dresses, eats all meals, answers and makes phone calls.

On her right side, an end table just large enough for a plastic tray with her meal du jour. At her left, a coffee tabletop filled with prescription medications, glass of water, letter opener, pens and pencils, scissors, phone lists, calendar, cell phone, bills to pay, numerous Christmas cards awaiting response.

She doesn't send Christmas cards but writes a personal response for each one she receives. There are two piles, those answered and those pending.

They bear postmarks from Paris, Cologne, Buffalo, Petersburg, Seattle, Holiday, Valencia, Tel Aviv, Phoenix. On the shelf below, an unwieldy clutter, largely untouched, of health newsletters, assorted books, dictionary, a hymnal.

Gisela makes notes on an oversized monthly calendar, reads mail, and writes letters and checks.

Across the room, her flat screen TV is turned on but mostly muted, except for local news, nightly network news, *Wheel of Fortune*, *Jeopardy!* and, because she always wanted to work in health care, *Chicago Med*.

Her jaw-length bob, more blond than gray, softens her rounded open face, and a broad ready smile draws others in, belying an unimaginably challenging life.

Most days find her in jeans and long tops or sweatshirts. White Adidas sport Kelly green laces she learned to make in a basement eight decades ago. She can't remember the last time she wore a skirt or dress.

A small kitchen lies a few steps to the right. The 30-second and one-minute buttons on a countertop microwave are nearly worn through their plastic coating. An oven provides storage for extra pans, too dirty to turn on, she says. An adjacent dishwasher is similarly unused.

Her refrigerator holds lox, liverwurst, brie, her favorite German bread. One drawer is used for fresh fruit, the other, for raw vegetables.

Wooden chairs at her kitchen table easily skid on the tile floor, making them unsafe for her tenuous footing.

Splayed legs, one shorter than the other, and painful knees make it difficult to walk any distance, even with her walker. But surgery is out of the question, too old, she says.

Clutter is everywhere. Books she plans to read, someday. Photos spanning decades. Briefly burned candles. Though her condo is small, her glass doors look out on the grassy expanse of a children's playground where rabbits chase each other around bushes and geese parade their young.

Beyond her interior hall door and the building's main entrance are well-trod sidewalks and manicured grounds. And it feels large enough.

A painted wooden trunk recedes into a corner of the crowded living room.

Blue, with a compass rose stenciled in white on the lid. It's largely obscured by a basket of yet-unused yarn on top. Inside are old pictures, and stories and poems she's written to make sense of her life. Her stories. Her truths. Her secrets. Stories yet unshared. Things best left unsaid.

Traditions

2

HAPPY BIRTHDAY—1940

Gisela wakes, yawns, stretches arms high overhead, imagining she can touch the ceiling. Then she smiles. This day belongs to her.

Sun streams through white lace curtains following days of oppressive fog, creating a warm glow in her bedroom. It gives the entire city an aura of freshness. *Kardinäle* whistle so clearly she thinks surely one has flown through her open window. Her father taught her to recognize their song, and Gisela can't wait to share her story with Sadie, who lives in the next block.

Today she will wear her favorite blue flowered dress with a white collar and a sash that ties behind her back, usually reserved for Mass.

Gisela opens her bedroom door and hears her mother singing softly, as she does every morning.

As she heads to her chair in the kitchen, her mother lights two white candles with a wooden match and places them in the middle of the table. They will burn all day until Gisela returns home, *Mutter* promises.

Her usual breakfast is porridge with yogurt. Today she also gets a slice of dark bread with a smear of butter and jam.

They'll sit for dinner promptly at 6 p.m., as always, Gisela, *Mutter* and *Vati* and little *Bruder* Rolf.

After dinner she sits in her wooden kitchen chair, holding tight to the edges of the seat, giggling as her father lifts her up three times, each time higher, higher, singing Gisela the birthday song.

Hoch sollst du leben,
Hoch sollst du leben,
Drei mal hoch, hoch, hoch!
Long may you live,
Long may you live,
Three times, cheers, cheers, cheers!
Her braids fly out with each lift. She loves that her fair hair and blue eyes match the coloring of her father.

The two candles still burn, as her mother said they would. She tells Gisela that one represents the light of her life, and the other, the years to come.

Rolf, who is three, claps as her mother and Gisela blow them out together. *Mutter* had written her name in blue frosting across the top of her birthday cake.

She is eight years old.

Earlier that day she gave each child in her classroom a piece of Moser-Roth chocolate wrapped in shiny blue foil the color of wild cornflowers. Her parents taught her the German tradition that when you celebrate a birthday, you give treats to others. *Vati*, she starts to say. Chocolate was scarce, and he had somehow found the rare treat for her to share.

She wants to tell him how excited her classmates were about her gift. Some unwrapped theirs, ate it right away, then asked for another piece; others slipped theirs into a pocket to save for later.

But she stops.

Speaking without first being spoken to could result in a slap across the face, even on your birthday.

She wants to be a good girl, to please her father and the nuns who teach her about sin.

Sin is talking back to adults or refusing to obey them, lying, taking something that doesn't belong to you, touching yourself between your legs or letting someone else touch you there.

Her mother is cutting her cake as her father leaves the kitchen to change back into his work uniform and hurry down the steps from their apartment building.

She can hear the hard strike of his leather-soled shoes growing fainter on the concrete. He is gone when her mother sings to her while pulling up the bed covers, *Guten Abend, Guten Nacht.*

Two days later, the Royal Air Force begins raining bombs on their hometown of Köln.

3

Afternoon Mail

After a routine nap in her recliner, Gisela prepares to check mail that is delivered late afternoon to a bank of boxes down the hall.

A walking stick on the floor next to the recliner helps lift her up. It's more stable than a cane, and the leather strap is embossed with tracks of animals which imprinted her life. Black bear, deer, coyote, all passed at times through the various wild patches she's called home. She likes to run her hands over the smooth hickory of the stick, thinking of other hands that cut, sanded and varnished it before it arrived at her home.

It reminds her of a time when hiking was a regular part of her life, up hillsides, along wetlands and on rocky beaches.

Once the stick would have been an accessory, now it provides support that eases her through the days as she navigates them alone.

She looks at the knots where branches emerged before they were broken off. Like her life, she thinks.

But it is her walker that accompanies her down the hall. Her bills still come in envelopes. Even when she had internet service, since canceled, she didn't trust anything online, least of all her bank account or credit card numbers.

One day in early spring she pulled a collection of envelopes and papers from her mailbox, tucked them under the seat of her walker, and brought them back inside her condo, laying them unread on the coffee table. First, she'd lay lox on bread spread with cream cheese and slice an apple into wedges. When people asked her secret for longevity and good health, she unfailingly answered positive thoughts, strong coffee, black, and seafood. Fresh Alaskan salmon when she could get it.

Gisela started rifling through the mail while still finishing her lox and apple.

She made two piles, saved mail returned to the coffee table, junk mail to the floor.

A weekly shopper with real estate listings—not in the market; puppies for sale—no thanks! To the floor.

Telephone bill with regular calls to family and friends in Germany, on the table.

A postcard from her congresswoman, whose name she can never remember, to the floor.

At the bottom of the pile, which she hadn't noticed at first, was a hand-written notecard with no return address. Her birthday was two months away. Picking up the paring knife she'd used to cut the apple, she sliced open the top, then set it aside to look at after she'd finished eating.

An Unexpected Guest

4

The Letter

It was a notecard with a big *J* on the front, from her great-granddaughter. Jessica's family is one of those which veers to one side. Christmas and family celebrations consist of her Italian father's extensive family of grandfather, aunts, uncles, and cousins. Gisela knows Jessica only slightly. She can't recall the last time they'd been in the same room.

"Dear Grandma,

Can I come visit you during spring break?

Love, Jessica."

Gisela turned the card over to see if more was written on the back. There wasn't. Spring break, when was that? Jessica mentioned no dates, nor how long she would stay. Why did Jessica want to visit her when they barely knew each other?

Jessica lives a state away. Gisela imagined she would stay overnight.

Gisela's routine didn't easily accommodate houseguests. Afternoon nap. Early bedtime. 1 a.m. rising for coffee and liverwurst on toast. Foot vibrator for neuropathy at 6 a.m. Prescription drugs spaced 30 minutes before breakfast.

What passed as her guest room was essentially a sofa bed in an alcove, with no door. Open to the lights Gisela turned on throughout the night, plus her frequent visits to the bathroom. It was littered with all the things she had no other place to store. Out of season and outdated clothes, boxes of old letters and postcards, an old computer monitor and keyboard she no longer used.

One day she'd sort and discard, she kept telling herself. Now she had who-knew-how-long to prepare. Boxes would slide, barely, under the bed. If she carefully folded them, her clothes could be piled along the rear corner floor of the closet.

Gisela sometimes wishes she felt closer to her grandchildren and great-grandchildren. They barely know her, and she knows little of their lives.

Even her own children feel distant. As a little girl she was taught that her highest calling, her duty, was motherhood.

She acknowledges, with some regret and guilt, they probably needed more time and attention than she gave them growing up. She often took on more than one job to provide for them. Waitress, bartender, housekeeper—jobs accessible to those with beginning English.

Gisela and her two daughters live in the same city. One comes by once a month for an hour to wash the kitchen floor, clean the bathroom and vacuum. She sees the other during their monthly date for a pedicure.

Their phone conversations are clipped.

"How are you doing?"

"I'm doing."

"What's new?"

"Nothing."

"Do you need anything?"

"No."

"Love you."

"Love you."

"Goodbye."

And always, she feels a need to shield them from her past, their past. Voices from years ago still occupy space in her head, those of her father, and of the one who claimed to be the real *Vater* of all children of the Third Reich, the *Führer* himself.

A child must have a name, *Vati* once told her. Those words circled endlessly through her mind, shaping her life for decades. Mothers protect and nurture, but it is fathers, whether present or absent, who cast the longest shadow. Boys and girls spend a lifetime striving to measure up to actual or perceived standards, ever seeking their father's approval as their lodestar. When a father is absent or unknown, he can be spun into a mythical character of boundless proportions. Sons would be him, daughters would fawn over him.

Sometimes Gisela agonizes over what she has done to her children. Then she brushes the thoughts aside and moves on.

It is friends who fill her life now.

Sunday mornings are reserved for her church. More than just a worship service, the church is her warm and embracing family. A half-hour drive away, she now rides with other members since reluctantly giving up her car.

She's known most members on and off for decades. Many are German like Gisela, with shared histories and memories, though services are conducted in English.

When a family from Colombia joined the congregation, she set out to learn a few words of Spanish because she remembers what it was like to be unable to converse with people around her.

After the service, there are handshakes and banter all around. They envelop each other in hugs. Frequent potluck meals and weekday lunches cement bonds over shared food.

Gisela sings with the church choir, her love of music echoing her mother's. Once a mezzo-soprano, her voice has morphed into alto with passing years.

She also joined a choral group in her housing complex. Her walker becomes her seat as fellow altos rearrange their chairs to accommodate her.

During a Christmas concert she led the choir in singing the first verse of *Silent Night* in German, and the crowded room stood as one in ovation.

At another concert she performed *You'll Never Walk Alone,* remembering and honoring the high school choir who sang it when she made her American citizenship. Moving her audience to tears.

This is my life, she says.

And now, Jessica. Stepping into, impinging on, the quiet alone time where Gisela dwells in comfort.

After taking her tray to the kitchen to wash her plate and glass, she returns to her recliner to make plans and write lists.

Food—she'll need enough for at least a few days.

A change of sheets for the bed, a new pillow to replace the existing one flattened to uselessness.

She had to find the surge protector power strip she used before getting rid of her computer and tablet.

Jessica would need it in her bedroom. She'd have a cell phone to charge, and maybe a tablet, too.

And just why was Jessica coming anyway? Why now?

Flowers & Chocolates

5

Jessica Arrives

Gisela rose even earlier than her usual 6 a.m., surveying her packed refrigerator as she pushed the button on the coffee maker.

"You done snorting and farting?" she says to no one but the pot itself, as it gurgles through its routine.

Her own breakfast would be brie cheese on toast, and leftover chicken soup. As she ate, she watched passing time on her wristwatch. Friends tease her about still wearing a watch, but she reminds them she already knows the time while they are still reaching for their cellphone.

9 o'clock.

Jessica had sent her arrival date on a postcard, though not the time she would leave home nor when she expected to arrive.

10 o'clock.

Promptness and timeliness, a certain orderliness, were deeply ingrained in Gisela from childhood.

Uncertainty made her uneasy. She'd already drained her coffee pot.

Late morning, after 11, she heard a loud knock. Both relieved and apprehensive, Gisela opened the door.

"Hi, Grandma," Jessica booms in a gravelly voice that Gisela finds slightly grating.

Jessica strides in wearing jeans roughed at the knee and a white tee emblazoned with a small Italian flag under the word ITALIA, and giant wrap-around sunglasses.

"What do you think, Grandma?" Jessica twirled around. "Do you like my Italian vibe?"

Gisela surveys Jessica's high cheekbones, her angular face, her brown eyes, her thick dark hair, and strains to see anything of herself, of her genes, in the teenager standing before her. A buxom figure, they did share that. Or once did, before age stole that from her.

"Welcome." A tepid, "I'm glad you're here."

"Thanks, Grandma. I'll just grab my gear from the car and be right back."

On her way back out the door, a framed vintage black and white photo of a young woman hanging eye-level in the hall catches her attention.

"Grandma, is that you?"

"*Ja.*"

"You were fire!"

"*Ja?*"

"I mean hot. You were beautiful."

"*Ja*, it was a gift and a burden." She stops. It was more than she meant to say.

Jessica returns with a beige backpack and an oversized black canvas tote with her name embroidered in red. Gisela points toward what will be her bed, and Jessica drops them on top.

"Did you eat this morning?"

"Just my homemade granola."

Despite her ambivalence about Jessica's visit, Gisela had planned a traditional German meal and beckons her to the kitchen table.

A platter is laden with assorted cheeses and sausages, artfully arranged in a circle.

Limburger, Munster, and Butterkäse cheese, interspersed with slices of summer sausage and liverwurst. On the side, dark bread, crackers, dill pickles, and two brands of mustard, Löwensenf and Hengstenberg, from her favorite German specialty store. Enough food to last through Jessica's stay, she reasoned.

Fresh flowers and chocolates sit on one end—quintessential elements of German hospitality. White carnations purchased from her grocery store, because they last longest.

German chocolates arranged on a small porcelain plate with forget-me-nots and gold trim around the rim. Hand-painted in Germany, she's carried it with her around the world.

"I should have told you before I came," Jessica says. "I'm vegetarian. You do know that sausage is filled with poisonous preservatives?"

"*Ja, Ja.* But I'm still here."

Still standing, Jessica picks up a piece of rye bread, covering it with a slice of Limburger and sharp mustard.

"I'm the only one in my family who likes Limburger. Once you get past the smell the taste is pretty mild."

Gisela gestures toward a chair for Jessica, then fills her plate and heads to the sanctuary of her recliner.

"Grandma, I've got great news. I'm going to school in Germany."

Gisela cocks her head.

"*Ja?* Germany?"

"I'm applying to their universities next year, and they require a Statement of Purpose. I need to write an admission essay of 1,000 words about my life and goals and why I want to enroll there."

"Not Italy? You're already dressed for it."

"Sorry, Grandma. I shouldn't have gone full Italian on you when I dressed this morning. I just got the tee on Etsy and was excited to wear it. But I came here to learn about my German side.

"I've asked my mother, but she says she doesn't know much. Only that her mother was born in Germany. That's why I'm here. I want to learn more.

"To hear your stories about growing up in Germany so I can include them in my essay. I'm a pretty good writer, and I think you'll like it. "

"My stories. You want to tell my stories."

Jessica reaches for a bunch of grapes.

Sounds of children's screams and laughter distract them, punctuating the air. Gisela often lets the music of children at play wash over her, thinking how different it is from the sounds of her own childhood.

"Did you know college is free in Germany, even for Americans? I took two years of German in high school and was best in my class. I'm graduating this spring."

"You want to write about my life."

I was right, Gisela thinks. She's going to ask about things best left unsaid. It's going to be a long day.

6

GROWING UP

"I wasn't sure about your internet service."

"I don't have any."

"I'm glad I brought a pad and pen. I'll grab it from my backpack."

Now it begins, Gisela sighs. She'd expected Jessica to return with a leather-bound journal, not one of those 89 cent notebooks on store shelves every August, before the school year begins.

"When I get home I can read my notes aloud, and my computer will save them in print. What was it like when you were my age? No, even before that, when you were a little girl."

"That was so long ago."

"What about your family?"

"Well, we ate our meals together. Not like today when everyone has their own schedule.

"Das Frühstück, Sieben. Mittagessen, Mittag. Abendessen, Achtzehn uhr."

"I know those words. Breakfast, 7 a.m. Lunch, noon. Dinner, 6 p.m. What else did you do together?"

"Vati would sometimes take me on long walks through our neighborhood, when he wasn't working."

Jessica opens her notebook and starts to write.

"He liked to take photos with his Leica. That's like the Mercedes of cameras."

"Or the Ferrari. I know about Leicas, Grandma. I know they were considered the best when cameras still used film, and now they make great digital cameras. I just use my cellphone."

"Sometimes he'd hold it low so I could look through the viewfinder with my right eye while I covered my left eye with my hand. One morning we saw a Great Spotted Woodpecker on an oak tree in our block. I saw it first—it had a red rump and a red patch at the back of its head. I started calling to it, but *Vati* warned me to be silent or it would fly away."

"Did it?"

"*Ja.* We'd walk everywhere. He'd focus on trees, flowers, shadows, raindrops, anything that caught his attention.

"I learned how and where to walk to and from my school even before I was old enough to attend. *Vati* had taught me how to take care of myself.

"On my first day of school, my parents gave me a *Schultüte.*"

"A what?"

"A big cardboard cone as tall as I was, filled with candy. Children still get them today, when they start school.

"I walked to and from school on my own from the very beginning."

Jessica looks up.

"My parents drove me to school for two years before they'd even let me take the bus alone."

"Children must learn how to be free."

"You said your dad loved nature."

"*Ja.* In summer we'd take the train to the Taunus Mountains to hike and breathe in fresh mountain air.

"My favorite thing was the wildflowers. We'd pick chamomile—they look like tiny daisies—to dry for tea.

"*Mutter* said it would help us relax and fall asleep. She made tea of wild mint to calm our stomachs. She knew a lot about herbs for healing."

"I like nature too, but herbs instead of medicine?"

"Herbs are medicine. German doctors and druggists, and health and wellness practitioners all use and prescribe natural medicines based on plants."

Gisela reaches toward her coffee table for a tube of Arnica cream.

"This has been used since the 1500s for sores and bruising and sore muscles. A nun, Hildegard von Bingen, wrote about it in the 12th century. Now you can buy it at Walmart. I rub it on sore muscles. It's made from the arnica plant, which has bright yellow flowers. I used to see it in the mountains.

"We also picked elderberries. They have antioxidants and vitamins that boost your immune system.

"*Vati's* favorite was birds. When we were in the mountains he introduced me to Common Swifts. They can stay in the air for 10 months without stopping.

"I thought that was amazing."

"We have a sunflower seed feeder in our yard but the only birds I really know are chickadees and bluejays. You lived in Cologne, right?"

"Köln. It's KUR-luhn. We lived in an apartment. Everyone I knew lived in an apartment building. Most families didn't have a separate house like you."

"Okay. KUR-luhn. Did you have friends nearby?"

"When I walked to school I'd pass Sadie's apartment in the next block and we'd walk together. We sat next to each other in class. Later she was assigned to a different school and had to walk in a different direction."

Secrets

7

My Untold Story—1938

Vati worked for the government, at the central train terminal downtown. I think he dispatched trains, though he never said and I never asked him. I know he was a Nazi, but I still can't make myself say the word, even to Jessica. It's so fraught with guilt, even today. Guilt glides down through generations, and I want to protect my children.

My father wore the uniform and armband of a Nazi, like everyone who worked for the Third Reich, and wore it proudly. He taught me the Nazi salute and told me his job depended on my doing it every time I walked into class or met an adult on the street or in a store.

I did it with gusto, dozens of times a day. Maybe even a hundred.

One night I woke up when my father came home late. I was only six, but from a gap in my bedroom door I could see his pants were torn and stained in red.

He was wearing a saber I had never seen before. That night would be called *Kristallnacht*, Night of Broken Glass. Jewish homes, synagogues and shops were attacked, looted, and burned, filling streets and sidewalks with shards of glass from broken windows. November 9, 1938. Some 30,000 Jewish men, from their teens to their 60s, were arrested in their homes and sent to concentration camps. I learned about it years later.

Was *Vati* a part of that? I never found out where he was or what he did that night. Nor why he had blood on his pants.

A week earlier, our teacher had called Sadie and me to a small table at the front of the room and told us to sit down facing the class. Starting with me, then Sadie, she pointed a wooden baton to our eyes, nose, mouth, and hair. She asked other students to compare our features to pictures in a book.

I started to tremble. Sadie crossed her arms and put her head down.

"Sadie, lift your head!" Frau Reitz rapped her baton on the table.

"Which one is the Aryan?" Everyone knew the answer. We heard the same lesson over and over.

"They are the special race who will carry Germany 1,000 years into the future," Frau Reitz said.

We returned to our seats, and after class walked home in silence, pretending it had never happened. The morning after *Kristallnacht*, Sadie wasn't outside to meet me. Neither was Levi, the boy who teased me about my long blond braids. Their fathers had been taken away, and Jewish children were barred from public schools.

Next to his camera, my father prized his A. Lange & Söhne silver pocket watch. I could look at it, but wasn't allowed to hold it or even touch it.

Each year, before the holidays, *Vati* had it cleaned and checked by Heinen, a fine mechanic and master watch repairer. His shop was near the Köln Cathedral.

Christmas Markets start in late November, and my family always went a few weeks later to a market in the square in front of *der Dom*. Its twin towers seemed to reach the angels, piercing the sky higher than I could see. I loved seeing my reflection in shiny glass ornaments and listening to music boxes.

Vati always bought me a marzipan pig for good luck. I saved it until Christmas Eve. Then I ate it.

Nazis tried to scrub Christmas and introduced a new hymn, *Exalted Night,* about motherhood, renewal, and holiday fires. Instead of Christmas, it celebrated Winter Solstice and a returning of daylight. The Christmas Market still sold figures of Mary and the Baby Jesus, but with blond hair and blue eyes. Aryan coloring. My coloring.

This year my father put his pocket watch in a kitchen drawer and never talked about having it cleaned by Heinen again.

"Shop closed," he said. "The monkey is sick."

8

BOMBS

Jessica picks at food, notebook in hand, strolling back and forth between kitchen and patio door. It's an uncommonly warm spring day, and life surges.

"So Sadie transferred to another school. You must have missed her. Grandma, weren't you alive during the war?"

"*Ja.* Wouldn't you like to sit down?"

Now it begins in earnest, Gisela thinks. Jessica probing her family history. My history.

Gisela hadn't talked about any of this in years and was not keen to do it now. Even as it was going on, you didn't speak of it. Some things were best left unsaid.

"Weren't you terrified?" Jessica asks in the shared disbelief of all who've never tasted war.

"We went on living."

Jessica pauses, notebook open, silently leaving space for Gisela to continue speaking.

Gisela measures how much to say next.

"After bombing started, we'd listen for air raid sirens and run down steps to a shelter in the basement."

"The basement?" Jessica is writing again.

"Coal bins were down there, and the dust made me cough and wheeze. Each family claimed their own space, but we were all close together. We had blankets and books and card and board games. My favorite board game was *Mensch*. If you've played Sorry! it's kind of like that.

"My brother and I were the only children, and our parents tried to keep us quiet. I had a flashlight, and I'd read and do homework under my blanket. My pencil lead kept breaking but *Vati* would sharpen it with his pocketknife.

"I've always liked to read. When I found books about America written in German, I started to imagine coming here.

"Wondering what it would be like to go to a place so far away."

"Do you remember any of the titles?"

"I wish I did.

"*Mutter* also taught me to knit socks and make shoelaces." She points to the laces in her Adidas.

"Did you know Adidas are German, too?"

Gisela hesitates.

"You probably know some of this from your history classes.

"Jews couldn't go to school with us anymore."

Jessica looks up.

"So Sadie had to move to another school?"

"Yes, to a Jewish school. I really missed her, especially walking together in the morning.

"One cold February night it was so beautiful my heart could barely contain it. Snow had fallen a few days earlier, then skies cleared on a full moon. After dinner we heard air raid sirens, and my father made sure electric lights in our apartment building were turned off.

"But moonlight on fresh snow made everything on the ground appear nearly clear as day.

"Bombs fell so close that even in our shelter we could hear them buzzing."

"My family has never talked about any of this."

"I never see your family. I'm not invited, even for Christmas."

Jessica stops writing and looks up.

"Would you come? I invite you now."

Gisela looks away.

"After it was over, we barely spoke of that night. It was time to move on."

9

My Untold Story—1942

Sirens warned us of incoming bombs. There were no elevators from our fourth-floor apartment to the basement. I learned to slide down the banisters and taught Rolf to follow me. It was much faster, and more fun.

Plaster walls in our apartment started cracking when bombing began, and with each explosion the cracks spread. After *Mutter* cleared and washed dishes from dinner, Rolf and I would brush our teeth and put on extra layers of clothing before going to bed. Pulling one stocking up my leg, and then another stocking on top of that, was really hard. *Mutter* would slip a second dress over my head as I still tugged at my stockings.

We'd need extra layers if we had to leave home in a hurry and didn't have time to grab other clothes.

No one cared if anything matched, or how we looked.

When all the extra layers were in place and my shoes were on the floor nearby, I'd flop on my bed. My job was to carry down a canvas bag with our birth certificates, marriage certificate, and extra cash.

We were already in the basement on that moonlit February night when I felt afraid for the first time. Then everything went black. The walls shook and we could hear the cellar door jam.

We were trapped inside!

After bombing stopped, neighbors heard our screams and helped pry the door open. When we climbed out of the basement, we could smell burning flesh. There were fires everywhere.

At first, we were relieved our building still stood. We raced up the four flights to our apartment and once inside found the windows had blown out and household goods and toys had all flown outside.

My mother was teaching me four hands piano; now it was just a spaghetti bowl of broken strings.

For years after I was too distraught to use any keyboard.

The next morning I learned that Sadie's apartment building was leveled. My best friend was dead.

Signs Everywhere

10

WHO KNEW?

"Jessica, I'm sorry for what I said about your family and Christmas. We live a long way apart."

"Grandma, that is the first time you have called me by name."

"Is it? Well, let's move on."

Jessica sighs and re-opens her notebook.

"What about the Jews? You must have known what was happening to them. You said Sadie was your best friend."

"We saw buses with black curtains over the windows, and we thought they carried travelers still asleep in the morning or evening. But that was how they transported the Jews."

"And you had no idea?"

"We found out much later."

"But there were signs everywhere.

"'Jews Forbidden.' 'Jews not Welcome.' I saw pictures on the Holocaust Museum website.

"And what was Aryan about? I never understood what that meant."

"We didn't pay attention. We didn't ask questions."

11

My Untold Story—1941

I walked past a construction site for a new office building on my way to and from school in Köln. A banner hanging from the scaffold said, "We have our Führer to thank that we are working here today. *Heil Hitler!*"

I saw the same sign on a fence by a school playground being enlarged for more children to practice marching. Posters said, "Germans, Your Enemy is the Jew."

I suppose I should have paid more attention, but I was just a child. My mother didn't believe in the Nazi government, I'm sure of that. She refused to say *Heil Hitler.* Even if I couldn't ask my father questions, I could have talked to her.

Being young did not save me from the guilt that's followed me all these years.

At the restaurant where our parents took me and Rolf on special occasions, a sign read, "No Jews Allowed."

The same signs were posted everywhere. When children tripped over a stone, we would say, "Oh, a Jew is buried there." I didn't think to connect any of it with Sadie. She was just my friend.

Decades after the war's end, Köln artist Gunter Demnig began a project called *Stolpersteine*, stumbling blocks. Brass plates engraved with the names of Nazi victims are attached to cobblestones in front of their last known address, to keep their names alive. Some 100,000 have been placed throughout Germany and 25 other countries.

Aryan had nothing to do with race, let alone a superior one. It was a scholarly term for groups of people who spoke related European and Asian languages thousands of years ago. But Nazis used it as a cover for separating Jews, Blacks, Gypsies, and Gays.

As time passed my father didn't laugh anymore and he was even stricter with us.

On our last Christmas Eve in Köln, traditional holiday music filled our home despite Nazi efforts to erase it. *Mutter* and I played *In Dulci Jubilo*, Good Christian Men Rejoice, on our piano and *Vati* played *Adeste Fideles* on the violin.

When family gifts were exchanged, my present was a doll with beautiful hair. Real hair. Later I would learn it was hair from a Jew.

A New Home

12

City Girl/Country Girl

"After bombing ended that night the trains were still running, and my mother and brother and I left the city by train. We stuffed a few belongings into a half-dozen suitcases and sacks. My father stayed behind to work."

Jessica is writing faster now.

"*Mutter* held us both close and made us feel safe. A half-day later we reached a small village where we would finish growing up. My parents thought surely Allied bombers wouldn't bother with a village of 500 people, and we would be safe there."

"But you left your home and best friend behind."

"Many families moved their children out of the city. A farm family said we could stay in a small house on their land.

"I worked for them, helping out in the fields and barn because their sons were away in the army."

"Your own house. Better than an apartment, right? What about school?"

"We started school right away. The village had a one-room school for eight grades. You went to chairs in the front of the room when your grade was called. The rest stayed at their desks to study. I had just finished fourth grade in Köln and I was at the same level as eighth graders in the village."

"No wonder I'm so smart! Was it anything like school in Köln?"

"Some things were the same. Every class started with a song. Most of them were about nature, a few were about the military. I liked singing together in a group. My mother loved music and so did I. I still sing in choirs.

"Here's something you can use in your admission essay. When I was 10 I had to join *Jungmädelbund*, the Young Girls League.

"After going to a couple of meetings and passing a physical fitness test you became a member the following April 20, on Hitler's birthday.

"Last year a friend came to visit me on April 20. My first words as she walked through the door were, 'It's Hitler's birthday.'"

"After all this time?"

"The words just tumbled out.

"In 1944, when I was 12 years old, I joined *Bund Deutsche Mädel*, the League of German Girls.

"We did sports, like the broad jump and track. I liked it and I was good. I even won some medals.

"Marching was a big part of belonging to Hitler Youth for both boys and girls. I'd put on my uniform, with a middy blouse, and a dark blue skirt. I was in this group one year before the war ended."

"So your life in the village sounds pretty good."

Gisela pauses, looks away. Far away.

"Yes, Jessica. Life was good."

Village Life

13

My Untold Story—1942

Our house was just a shack with one room stacked on the other. We stored vegetables in a small root cellar that was filled with spiders and bugs—I hated it. The bathroom was an outhouse nearby, though in bad weather it felt like a mile. A single faucet became our kitchen, along with a wood stove for heat and cooking.

We all slept on the upper floor. *Mutter* strung rope at one end to hang our uniforms. My uniform was the only outfit I had, except for a dress I wore to school every day. I tore it once, and *Mutter* mended my dress several times. I wore shoes that were too big for me and had holes in the soles.

I put layers of newspaper inside to keep my feet dry. I changed the papers several times a day, especially on rainy days and in winter.

With nowhere else to move, we lived there through the war and beyond.

Besides marching, we wore our uniforms at memorial services for each of our many soldiers who died on the front. I knew families who lost one, two, even three sons in the war. Our teacher started and directed a choir that performed at the services, and I sang soprano.

In place of rent, I helped the farmers who owned our house. I learned how to plant and harvest, how to mow grass and turn it in the sun by hand so it would graduate to hay, how to milk cows and churn the cream to butter, how to lead a team of oxen, how to shovel and spread manure—farm work that the men would have done had there been no war. They loaned me clothes from their sons when I had to work in barns.

After a day in the field my back started hurting, the beginning of back problems that have followed me through life.

Food was scarce. When I could eat with the farmers my mother needed less food at home.

They always had bacon gravy and baked potatoes.

Everybody grabbed potatoes and dipped them in the gravy. That was dinner, at least it filled your tummy. My pay for helping in the house for one afternoon was usually a liter of fresh milk, a few eggs, sometimes fresh baked bread and some fruit. *Mutter* was grateful when I could earn that.

I also had to perform a *Pflichtjahr*, a year of duty. I was assigned to a young couple who owned a flour mill and restaurant about four kilometers south of our village, to help them however needed.

Chickens and pigs had to be tended, and there was always work in the mill and in the house. The restaurant was not busy because of the lasting food shortage, but travelers sometimes filled beds overhead and rooms needed cleaning.

No one had an automatic washer. Laundry was boiled in a large copper kettle, scrubbed on a washboard, and rinsed by hand.

Then we spread it out on the lawn to bleach, rinsed it again, and hung it on the clothesline to dry.

There was no cleaner smell than that of freshly dried laundry.

During that year my only free time was every second Sunday afternoon. That's when I walked home through the woods to see *Mutter* and Rolf. I would hear noises and wonder what bird or animal was nearby. A badger? A hedgehog? A deer? A wild boar? My imagination excited me and I hoped for a glimpse of whatever it was.

Years later, when I worked in an American department store, I met a woman who was sent to a home in the country for safety when she was only five years old.

Her parents didn't imagine she would be beaten for not doing simple tasks fast enough, and that she would be living in a whore house where abortions were performed. She never saw her father again; he was killed in a concentration camp. She didn't even know they were Jewish.

When our teacher entered the classroom in our village, everyone stood and raised their right arm.

He would say, "For the *Führer* a triple victory." We answered with a chorus of "*Heil*" three times.

During the first hour of school, we were taught about German history and what it meant to be a Nazi. We learned about new military victories. The Reich developed a radio, the *Volksender*, that every home could afford. One stood on the teacher's desk so we could listen to Hitler every time he spoke. Excerpts from *Mein Kampf* were also read in schools. I wanted to go to college and work in healthcare, but education for girls was limited to only 10 percent of all students, so my dream was unfulfilled. Girls were only to be wives and mothers. I call it *Zurückgehalten*, held back.

Hitler was everywhere. He looked over us from a portrait on the wall next to the blackboard. I still hear his voice in my ear. Shrill. Loud. But amid music and cheering, he had a voice that could draw you in and make you want to listen. His power came from his gifts as a speaker.

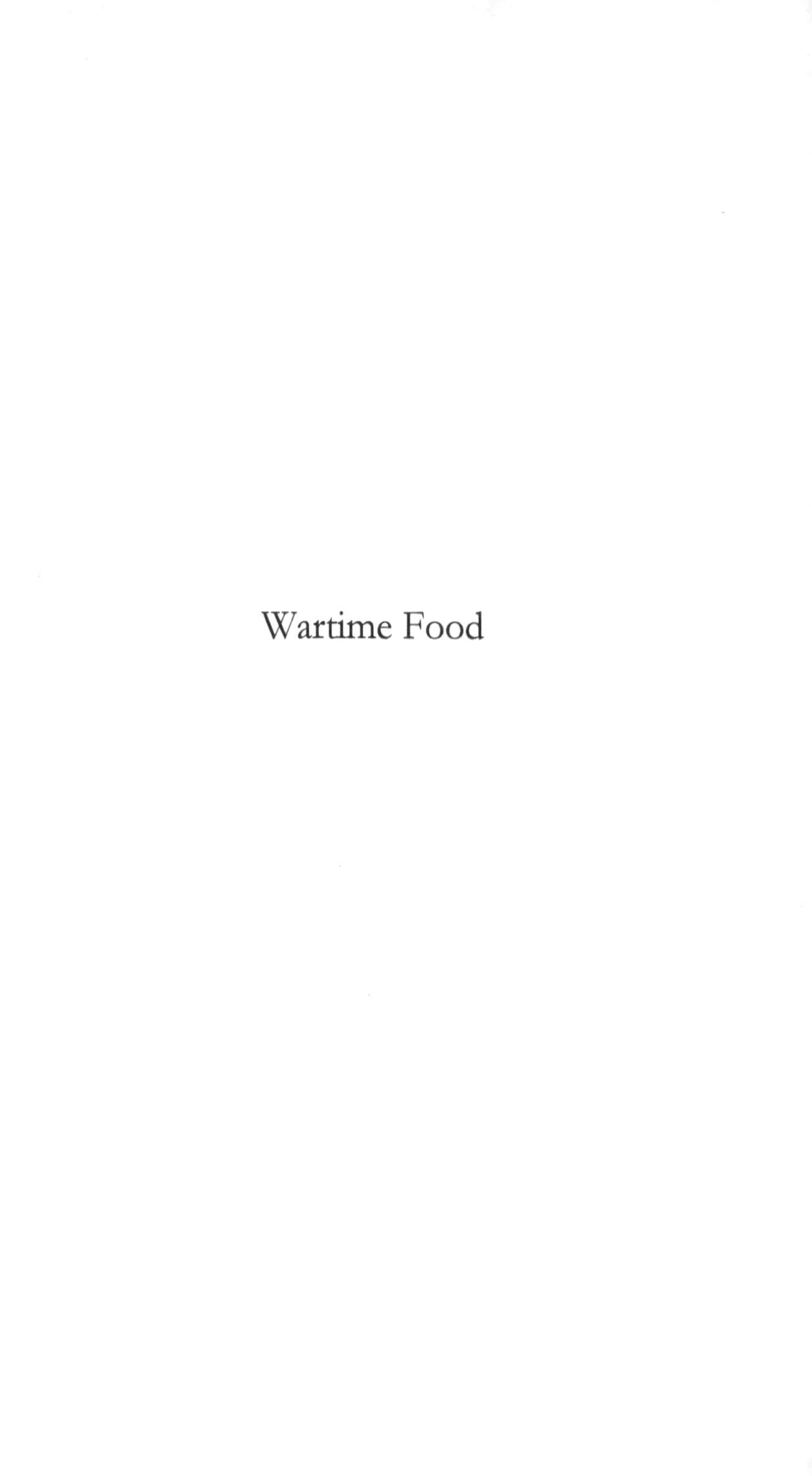

Wartime Food

14

No Time for Fun

Wanting more, Jessica presses on.

"I know you were in school, and marched and did sports in a youth group, but what did you do just for fun?"

"Fun? Fun? There was no time for fun! I was either working or in school."

Jessica reaches toward a bag of Riesen chocolates on the kitchen counter.

"No chocolate either. And nobody loves chocolate like Germans do. You can add this to your essay. We couldn't get coffee so we brewed roasted grains and acorns. We gathered twigs and pinecones in the forest to start a fire in the stove. We chopped firewood to stoke it.

"Our village had no grocery stores. Small shops sold baked goods or meat or supplies.

"You had to have a ration card, *Lebensmittelkarte*, to shop."

"Why are German words so long?"

"*Ja*, long as a freight train. My mother would stand in line, and by the time she got to the front, many times there was nothing left to buy. On Saturday we'd hang around the farmers' market hoping we could buy a loaf of home-baked bread. Feeding troops came first. Our daily allowance was a slice of bread, one potato, milk on some days, and meat only on Sundays, if you could get it."

"Do you still eat potatoes? I don't think I could face one ever again."

"I eat bread and potatoes almost every day. Mashed potatoes are my favorite, but boiled and fried too."

"What about fruit?" Jessica made a fruit smoothie every day of banana and blueberries or whatever other fruit was in the house. "I couldn't live without fruit."

"Fruit was mostly reserved for soldiers.

"We were luckier than people in Köln because we had land to plant a vegetable garden.

"We grew onions and potatoes and carrots, and cabbage *Mutter* made into sauerkraut."

"My mom has a little garden. She grows tomato plants in pots for fresh salsa, and some basil for pesto. Last summer we started a strawberry patch. But we're too busy for a real garden. We go to the farmers' market in town."

"Even long before the war, Hitler came up with the idea of *Eintopf*, a simple stew made in one pot. He decreed that the first Sunday of the month should be *Eintopfsonntag*, one-pot Sunday, when Germans gave up their traditional dinner of meat and potatoes."

Jessica starts writing again.

"Well as a vegetarian, I think that's a good thing."

"*Ja*. Hitler was a vegetarian too. He said everyone should eat a simple dish made of home-grown German food like the potatoes and carrots we grew in the village.

"He thought eating the same one-pot dish at the same time across the country would unite us as one people."

"Grandma, we make one-dish meals too. We use a Crock Pot!"

"*Ja*, if Hitler only knew it was invented by a Jew."

"No!"

"*Ja*. In the 1800s Jewish families in Lithuania prepared for Sabbath by putting meat, beans, and vegetables in their crocks on Fridays before nightfall. They took the crocks to local bakeries, to place them in ovens that were still hot and slowly cooled overnight. By morning, the low-and-slow residual heat would create a stew."

"Rad."

"An electrical engineer in America heard about this custom from a relative. He was always inventing something, and he created a slow cooker for his family so they could prepare meals without using the oven in summer heat.

"He applied for the patent in 1936. It was granted in 1940, during the same time Nazis were promoting one-pot meals in Germany.

"When he sold his business a couple decades later, they rebranded it as the Crock Pot."

"That's a great story, Grandma."

"When you go into restaurants in Germany you will still find one-dish meals on the menu. *Eintopf* lives on there, and in my slow cooker. I regularly throw in whatever I have in the refrigerator. Just as Hitler would have wanted."

It Was Over

15

WAR'S END

Gisela started to reveal more of her life during the war. But not too much, she hoped. Not yet. Maybe never. Jessica kept taking notes.

"Within two years after we moved to the village, Allies were moving closer. Everyone could tell the war was going badly for us.

"Early one morning *Mutter* gathered dry branches and newspapers and threw them in a burn barrel at the far edge of our garden. Then she lit a match and dropped it in. She had told me this day might come, and what I needed to do. 'Bring the papers,' she said. 'Hurry!'"

"So you already knew what she wanted?"

"*Ja.* I raced up the steps to a hiding place under old clothes on our second floor.

"I grabbed the same papers I had carried from our Köln apartment to the bomb shelter for safekeeping years earlier, birth certificates and marriage license.

"I added them to the fire, along with our copy of *Mein Kampf*."

"You had a copy of *Mein Kampf*?"

"Every German family had one. I don't think many people read it. It was 700 pages long. Copies were everywhere. People gave them as wedding and birthday gifts. *Vati* got one as an award from his boss. I read it front to back in school."

"Seven hundred pages. That's impressive! How much do you remember?"

"*Kein*. None. I put that all behind me.

"There was another book in most households, right next to *Mein Kampf* on the bookshelf. *The German Mother and Her First Child*. The author said mothers should ignore their baby's crying; they should be fed, bathed and dried off and otherwise left alone. Boys, especially, should be raised with no emotional attachment, to better serve the *Führer*."

"That is cold!"

"*Mutter* didn't believe in either book, and definitely not one about how to raise us."

"Did it go in the burn barrel too?"

"It blew out the window when we were bombed in Köln. A neighbor gave it to my mother when my brother was born.

"Radios ran day and night as people listened for news of the war. Every home and office had a wireless to carry Hitler's speeches. On April 30, 1945, I remember it was a Monday, the wireless broadcast, 'German men and women, soldiers of the armed forces: Our Führer, Adolf Hitler, has fallen.'

"People in our village ran onto the streets. They were all stunned. Someone asked, 'Should we do something?' Several said, 'I hated him. I'm glad he's gone.' No one mentioned mourning him."

"Didn't he shoot himself?"

"*Ja*, the broadcaster said he died defending our nation and the successor he named would be taking over.

"They didn't tell us that Hitler took his own life in his underground bunker."

"Meanwhile, your burn barrel was still smoking?"

"It was ashes by then. Now other villagers were lighting bonfires to destroy their own documents and copies of *Mein Kampf* like we did.

"Soon there was a haze of smoke over the whole village. A few days later we saw American soldiers coming toward us.

"Every house hung a white cloth in sign of surrender.

"It was over."

16

My Untold Story

Two weeks before Germany surrendered, my mother received a summons from Gestapo to report to a neighboring village with my brother and me.

"We're not going," she said.

The day after German surrender, my mother told me to sit down. She put her hand on my shoulder and looked me directly in the eye. *Mutter* said she had something important to tell me.

Something that even my father did not know.

Her grandfather was an Italian Jew, and her mother was considered Jewish and what was then called illegitimate.

That made *Mutter* half Jewish.

Her refusal to answer that summons, plus the American liberators, likely saved our lives.

Sidewalks

17

AFTERMATH

"Jessica, how about a walk outside? It's a beautiful afternoon. We can talk as we go."

"I'll get a jacket." Jessica walks over to her bed and reaches into her tote for an ivory fleece zip jacket.

Gisela lifts a sweatshirt from the back of her recliner—the front reads *Grand Canyon*—and eases it over her head.

Stiff from sitting, she pulls herself up with her walking stick, reaching for her walker a few steps away. Her walker also serves as a seat, which she'll use while Jessica joins her frequent breaks on park benches scattered along the sidewalks.

On the way out her door she picks up her condo key on a lanyard and hangs it around her neck.

Her condo is at one end of the building, and doors leading to the outdoors are close by.

Two doors later, they emerge into the late afternoon sun.

"Did you go back to Cologne after the war ended, Grandma?"

"Köln! Remember? It's Köln. There was no Köln to return to. Köln was a ghost town. It was bombed over 260 times. Everything was rubble. More than half of the houses and public buildings were destroyed, most others were damaged. There was no gas, no water, no electricity, no transportation. Bridges across the Rhine collapsed."

They'd barely started their walk when they met Sally with Scout, her poodle mix.

"Good afternoon, Gisela. Who is this?"

"My great-granddaughter, Jessica."

"Hi cutie," Jessica bends over to greet Scout. She finds a dog cookie in her jacket pocket.

"May I give it to him? I have a beagle mix we adopted at a shelter. I miss her already."

Sally wanted to know where Jessica was from, and all about her visit.

Five minutes later, Gisela said it's time to move on. A park bench was a short distance away.

"I need to sit down on my walker. You can have a seat on the bench."

Jessica scrolls through emails and texts as Gisela starts talking with a man walking slowly by.

"Hi, Steve. This is my great-granddaughter, Jessica. Where's Anne this afternoon?"

"Feeling a little weak. The doctor said she has early Parkinsons."

"I'm so sorry, Steve. Let me know if I can do anything for either of you."

Jessica stops scrolling and looks up with a sympathetic smile.

Remembering her packed refrigerator, Gisela says, "I could bring you something to eat. You let me know how she's doing."

He smiles and waves as Gisela slowly rises to continue their walk.

"Jessica, it's important to help someone whenever you can. I'm ready to start walking again.

"Look, daffodils are already in bloom. You should see these flowerbeds in summer. Flowers in every size and color, and not a weed in sight. I'd like to show you a pond next to the playground."

"You're taking quite a walk today, Gisela." It was Harold and Lucille, out with their Golden Retriever. Gisela subconsciously backs away. She doesn't like any dogs, least of all one as big as their Aspen. Why did people want dogs anyway? Jessica reaches in for another cookie, though it's barely a tidbit for 65 pounds of dog.

"We enjoyed your talk at the senior center last week," Lucille says. "We had no idea of all that you went through during the war, and even after it was over." They nod and walk on.

Jessica looks straight at Gisela.

"What did you tell them about, Grandma?"

Gisela ignores her question and returns to their previous conversation.

"You were asking me about returning to Köln before we saw all these people.

"Somehow my father found a place to live near our old neighborhood and moved back after the war.

"Once we rode a freight train to visit him, and I didn't recognize any of the streets we once walked together."

Her neighbor from down the hall is walking her rescue dog of mixed who-knows-what breed. "I've never liked that dog," Gisela mutters to Jessica, recoiling as they approach and Mopsie sniffs each of her legs.

Mopsie shifts her attention to Jessica, who holds the back of her right hand to the dog's nose while scratching behind her ear with the left.

"Why don't you like dogs, Grandma?" Jessica asks after they've moved on.

"Never did. Here's a funny story. You know about Barbie dolls?"

"Sure, but I never had one. I thought they were kind of weird."

A breeze catches them both. Jessica shivers and zips her jacket.

"The original Barbie was based on a German-language comic book character. The Bild Lilli doll wasn't a toy, she was a popular gag gift guys gave each other. The Aryan ideal with her blond hair, blue eyes, and pouty look and buxom figure.

"Just like me." Gisela laughs.

In her great-grandmother's laughter, Jessica senses a chink in the wall dividing them.

"Some years after the war, the co-owner of Mattel toy company saw one in Europe. She persuaded her husband to manufacture them for little girls and named the doll after their daughter. The rest is history."

"It's good to see you out today, Gisela." It was Herb and Edith, taking their dachshund for his daily walk.

"What's his name?" Jessica asks.

"*Schatz.*"

"Darling. That's a sweet name for a German dog," Jessica says. "Is everyone who lives here German, Grandma?"

"No, but a lot are."

Schatz, in true dachshund form, barks and tugs at his leash, trying to reach one of the resident squirrels. Jessica finds one last cookie in her pocket before they move on.

"There's Fritz and Ida." Gisela waves to a couple across the street. *"Wie geht's?"*

"How do you know everyone? The only neighbors I know are my classmates."

"Sidewalks, Jessica. The difference is sidewalks. Walking, looking up and saying hello when you meet someone. That's what our society has lost.

"The pond is too far for today. Let's head back toward home."

"You said you went to visit your dad but didn't recognize anything."

"My parents were divorced by then. I was growing up, and really wanted a new dress.

"My father looked at my changing figure and gave me money and directions to a small dress shop that had opened amid the rampant destruction.

"Oh, hi Ben."

Another of her neighbors was walking by.

"I used to rent his garage."

"Tell me about the dress you bought, Grandma."

"It was blue, kind of medium blue, that's always been my favorite color. It had a fitted bodice and a full skirt that moved when I twirled around."

"And where did you think you would wear it?"

"I wasn't sure at the time, I just knew I was ready to start living.

"Jessica, you're looking forward to college in Germany. Don't you want to talk about your future instead of my past?"

"The past shapes the future, Grandma. I want to hear more about the war and how you survived. What you said at the senior center. You have made it sound too easy."

Gisela sighs.

"The war may have ended with a whisper, but it was far from over.

"In some ways everything changed, in some ways it felt like everything was the same, only worse.

"Food was even scarcer after the war ended."

"How so?"

"Because it could no longer be seized from countries the Nazis had occupied. Chocolate was unknown, meat could not be eaten every day. Coffee was not available. Store shelves were still empty."

"What did people say about the war?"

"No one spoke of it. The past was taboo. When children were old enough to ask their parents what they did during the war, they were met with silence.

"Or they were told, 'We suffered too.'"

No wonder no one in their family knew anything about her great-grandmother's past, Jessica thinks. Her great-uncle Leonardo was an American pilot during the war, and he didn't talk about it either. He had even sent home a German helmet with a name written inside in pencil that they couldn't read.

Years later her mom would say the soldier was still someone's son, someone's brother.

"We stayed in the village, the soil started to warm, and we continued gardening."

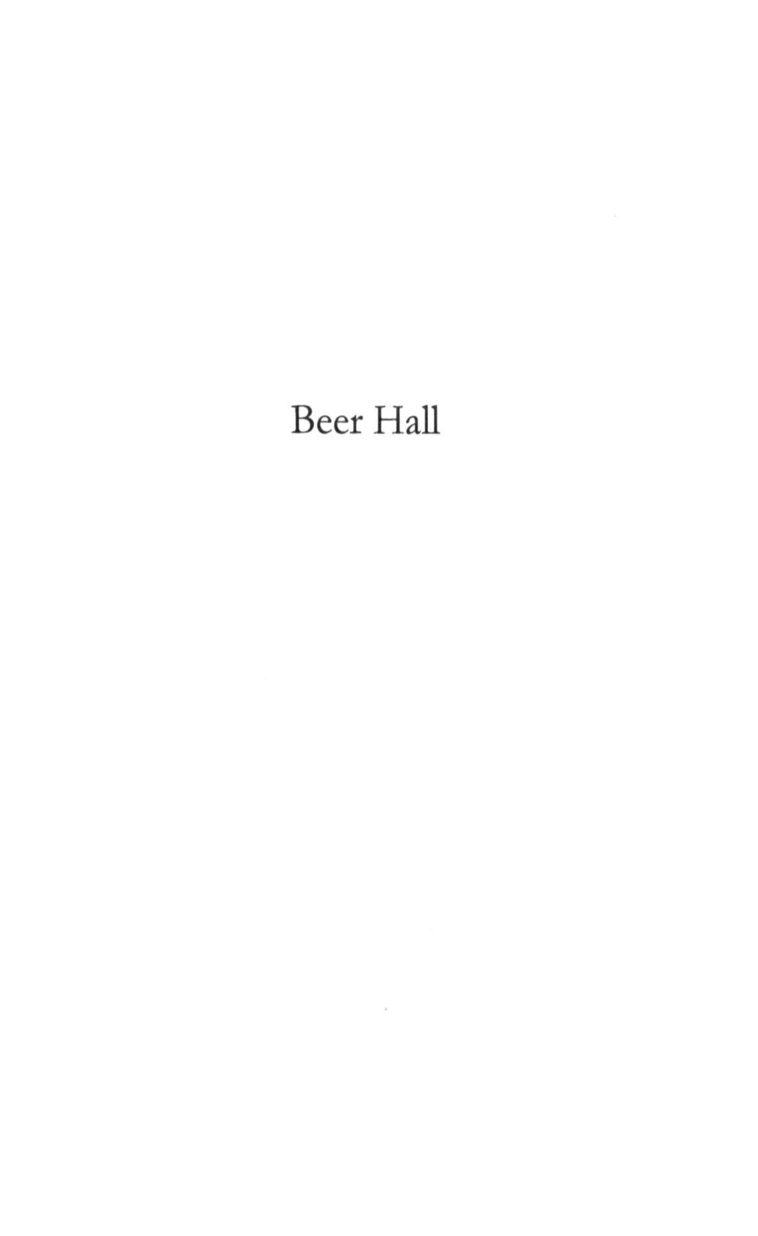

Beer Hall

18

THE OCCUPATION

Gisela was saying more than she had intended, maybe things she would regret.

"After the war, we were surrounded by American soldiers. They were everywhere. At first, they had orders to keep their distance. As time passed they were encouraged to mix with local residents, to help rebuild Germany. And mix they did. Many went home with German wives."

"How about you, Grandma? How did you feel about the American soldiers?"

"I was tired of everything. The boring food. Our dreary house. Many of our young men came back missing limbs, many others didn't come back at all.

"One evening I just decided to go to a dance at a beer hall. I knew that women who flirted with the Americans were called loose.

"I was just 17, shy, and didn't know a word of English.

"When I opened the door, Frank Sinatra's *Always* was playing on a jukebox, and the air was solid with cigarette smoke and the scent of beer. Most of the people inside were American soldiers."

"Did anyone ask you to dance?"

"I barely knew how to dance. When did I ever have time to learn? But a good-looking soldier patiently taught me a few steps and we tried to speak a few words. He had a warm smile and we laughed together at our attempts to communicate."

"So did you see him again?"

"*Ja.* We went to another dance. Even though I didn't know English and he knew only a few words of German, I could tell he was talking about America. It was like a dream I had since reading under my blanket during bombing raids."

19

My Untold Story—1950

It was just a dance.

My father, who once took me on long walks and taught me names for birds and flowers, no longer seemed to exist. The father who once had a sense of humor no longer laughed. He was strict, then harsh and then absent from my life. I longed for male attention and approval.

Hitler understood that longing. The *Führer* told children he was their real *Vater*, to solidify their future loyalty.

I suppose some people would call me a slut, and maybe I was. I touched my wrists with perfume, forced a shy smile, and gingerly opened the door into the beer hall. Inside, I happily melted into the warm arms of the American GI who had smiled back.

Leaning my face close to his, we swayed to music, exchanging words that neither could understand. So this is how it feels, I thought, sensing arousal deep inside. This is how love begins.

Twice after that, we went dancing. Once I wore the blue dress with the swing skirt from Köln. The last time, after we left the hall and I'd already had a few beers, he poured me a glass of vodka from a bottle in his car. I remember following him into a wooded area nearby, dropping onto the ground with him, and even through my alcohol haze, wondering how something that seemed wrong could feel so good.

I always knew I was meant to be a mother. The Third Reich taught me that while I was still a child myself. My GI was transferred back to the States shortly, never knowing he had fathered my first child, Jessica's grandmother. I never saw him again.

My brother was still at home and I didn't want to burden my mother with another child, so I took the train back to Köln to ask my father for support.

"*Raus aus meinem Haus!*" he shouted when I told him why I had come. "Get out of my house!"

I was 18 and alone. I asked everyone I met on streets and in stores, "Do you know of a place to stay?"

When I heard of a boarding house on the far edge of Köln, I set out walking, as I did so often in the village.

There was one empty room. I gratefully moved in but soon noticed a string of men coming in and out. So many of them. It was a whore house.

I walked back to my father's apartment. This time he relented and said something I've heard him whisper in my ear ever since.

"A child must have a name."

He was having an affair with a woman who had a grown son. Though I never understood why, her son agreed to marry me, to give my child his name.

We traveled by train back to my mother's house, and though we barely knew each other, we walked to a neighboring village and got married.

Two weeks later, with the help of a local midwife, I gave birth on the floor of the house where I'd lived since we were bombed out of our Köln apartment.

I thought it would be hard, but my labor was short and delivery, easy. For years I'd been told about the glories of being a mother, and now I was one. I was excited.

Soon after, we returned to Köln to live with his mother. Between being very pregnant and then recovering from giving birth, we never consummated our so-called marriage.

It did not take me long to realize I could never adapt to their lifestyle, and got an annulment. I packed up a box of belongings and the baby I'd named Petra, and returned to my mother's home.

20

A New Job

"Let's go back inside, Jessica. It will be cooler soon. Ready for a light supper?"

Returning to the kitchen, Gisela reaches in a drawer for clean blue and white plaid napkins. They were more economical than burning through paper ones. Using one to line a basket, she fills it with more assorted crackers, bread sticks, and slices of rye and sourdough bread. Green and black olives co-mingle in a glass bowl. Tearing spinach leaves, she adds chopped red onion and orange and yellow peppers, tossing in broccoli and sliced cucumber and radishes, and topping the salad with boiled egg slices, grated cheese and homemade Italian dressing.

For herself, Gisela takes out a few slices of salami to eat on crackers. Her house, her sausage.

Glasses of ice water would fill in for her usual glass of wine tonight.

"Do you mind if we watch *Jeopardy!* while we eat?" Gisela needed a break from what felt like an exhausting conversation.

Gisela got two correct answers in the *Jeopardy!* game show, an exceptional night.

"Ever think of applying to be on the show?" she asks after Jessica scored five right answers.

"Maybe, someday. I'll wash dishes."

In short order, Gisela returned food to the refrigerator and set up coffee for the morning, pouring water into the well and inserting filter and ground coffee.

"What about the guy you met at the dance?"

Gisela had hoped she'd forgotten about him by now.

"He was transferred back to the States, and I never saw him again."

"You said you were ready to start living. Did you find a way out of the village?"

"Soon after. Remember I said I learned to knit in the bomb cellar? I was fast and I was good.

"My first job was with a boutique that sold knit clothing. I knit skirts, pants and jackets for them. One day I was walking down a street and saw a display of my work in a shop window, and what they were charging customers compared to what they paid me. I quit that day."

"Good for you."

"I'd always wanted to work in health care, and I found a job with a pediatric hospital in a city some distance away. I rented a room from a doctor and his wife and stayed in the city on weeknights. On weekends I went home to *Mutter* and Rolf. There was still no good public transportation. I had to walk two and one-half hours on the side of the road each way."

"I can't believe how you just walked everywhere."

"There was no other way. Rolf was only 13. I worked so we'd all have money to help support us in the village."

Growing Family

21

My Untold Story—1954

Walking five hours between home and work every weekend was exhausting. It wasn't an easy walk. I'd have to step over uneven ground and big stones well off the shoulder. Sometimes vehicles veered off the road trying to avoid broken asphalt.

Late one afternoon, a sunny fall day, I felt drained by an unusually hectic week as I walked home. I thought of Petra constantly while I was away at work. I wished I could be the one who cared for her, not my mother.

But my salary helped *Mutter* and Rolf, and my work at the hospital gave me access to medical supplies. I got infant formula for Petra—it was first developed by a German chemist in 1865.

As I headed toward our village, an open Jeep with two American soldiers slowed.

The soldier on the passenger side leaned out and offered me a ride. He was friendly and I was happy about the idea of getting home to Petra faster.

I eased quickly into the back seat and the driver pulled away. Shortly he pulled off the main road onto a forest trail. I tensed, knowing immediately I'd made a huge mistake. I couldn't escape the car, and the soldier who offered me a ride raped me in the back seat while the driver watched.

When the war was over, many Russian soldiers assaulted German women. But Americans were our protectors, weren't they?

After they pushed me from the car and drove away, I ran into the forest, panicked. What if they came back and shot me?

I knew the forest well, but now everything felt unfamiliar. I was hiding when I heard them return, and they couldn't find me.

When I was sure they'd left I continued my walk home and told no one what had happened.

Nine months later I gave birth on our kitchen table. This time I had long, hard labor. A neighboring midwife, the same one who helped deliver Petra, eased my son's head out with forceps. He was very frail, and we took him to a hospital that was still short on staff and supplies after the war.

During one of my visits I could tell he was gravely ill and not getting the care he needed. I was sure Klaus would die there. I unhooked needles and tubes, grabbed him, and strode out the hospital's front door. My mother nursed him back to health and continued to care for Petra while I looked for another job.

The face of the soldier who raped me is seared into my memory, and years later I could see how much my son looks like his biological father.

Moonlight

22

FULL MOON

"I'm tired, Jessica. Could we continue talking in the morning?" Gisela gestures toward her bedroom.

"Me too."

First Jessica walks back to the glass doors for a view of the clear night sky.

"Grandma, come look at the full moon."

"Oh, I don't care about an old moon."

Gisela couldn't look directly at a full moon. Not ever. Not since the indelible memory of that terrifying night, with a full moon reflecting on fresh snow, lighting the way for Royal Air Force bombers.

For Gisela, holding tight to her stories, there would be little sleep tonight.

New Country, New Language

23

Coming to America

Gisela quietly used the bathroom, trying not to awaken Jessica, then went into the kitchen to turn on the coffee. Despite her efforts, Jessica soon joined her in pajamas, ready to resume last night's conversation.

"What do you have for fruit?" she asks, opening the refrigerator to reach for the container of Greek yogurt.

"In the crisper drawer. There's a banana in the freezer for a smoothie."

Jessica picks out fresh blueberries. Gisela had already laid a rubber spatula and drinking glass by the blender.

"Would you like an orange?"

None were available during the war. Now Gisela usually keeps them in the house.

December oranges were best—they were the biggest and juiciest and cheapest.

"No thanks."

"Do you need to contact your parents? Do you drink coffee?"

"Yes and no. I'll text them after we eat."

Texting, texting, whatever happened to old-fashioned phone calls, Gisela wonders. She toasts rye bread and tops it with mashed avocado—surely Jessica would approve.

"So did you stay with that job in the children's hospital or find something closer?"

"I did find another job, in a doctor's office closer to home. I also met Wayne, another American soldier among many still occupying Germany. He was good-looking, taller than me, with brown hair and a self-confident smile.

"He made me feel special, the way he showed me off in the service club where he was often first to order a round of drinks. He spoke only a few words of German, and I knew only a little English.

"When he asked me to marry him, I said yes. I thought my dream of America was finally coming true."

"How can you marry someone when you can't even talk with them?"

"Jessica, there is more than one way to communicate."

"Grandma, TMI!"

They both laugh, another small tear in the wall between them.

"We gradually learned from each other, between his English and my German. Wayne and I were engaged for three years when he was transferred stateside. I was still working when he left but he gave me some money to live on and told me to come to the States later."

"So how much later did you come? Is he my great-grandfather?"

"I got a letter from him in English that I couldn't read, so I threw it away. I never heard from him again. By then I'd met Bryce, a Master Sergeant.

"He was quieter and more intense, like my own father. Bryce was from New York and talked so much about his home state that I began to call him 'New York.' I was picking up a few more words of English. Bryce was good to my mother and little brother, and they both liked him."

"Was he a keeper?"

"Bryce and I were married in a small church in our village, with just my mother and brother there. I wore a simple blue dress; we didn't have money for a real wedding dress or even flowers. American soldiers who had been occupying West Germany since the end of the war were gradually being sent back home, and we were soon among them. We came to the United States on a troop carrier. Me and what felt like a thousand GIs.

"It was nine exhausting days at sea.

"I got so sick from the rough seas that I was hanging over the rail most of the trip. My hair was long and blowing in the wind. The vomit caught in my hair and came flying back into my face!"

"Ew! The cruise from hell."

"Then the Statue of Liberty came into view."

"And what did that feel like?"

"I thought, 'I'm really here.' It was October 4, 1957. I still remember the date.

"We spent one night in the Waldorf Astoria in New York City after we arrived. I was so tired I fell asleep in the elevator on the way up to our room. The next day my husband bought a car and we started driving across the state. He was so happy to be stationed at Fort Drum, New York. He thought New York was the center of the universe.

"During the war German prisoners of war were housed there, and some stayed after they were freed. It felt like a touch of home. We shared a guilt about the war that does not go away.

"I was happy to be out of Germany, there was still so much destruction, but I felt guilty about leaving my family too. So much guilt."

"How did you adjust to living in a new country? I think about that a lot.

"At least I've learned some German."

"*Ja*, language is important. We had a black and white television set in our apartment, and it was my best English teacher.

"Not the programs, but the commercials. I matched words to pictures, listening to them over and over and over. Some were quite long, telling a story in pictures and words."

"Great idea, Grandma. No internet to help you then."

"There were a lot of car commercials for GI families building homes in new suburbs. When I watched a commercial for Volkswagen, I thought, 'Am I in America?' Hitler promoted it as the 'people's car' that every German could afford.

"I got a waitress job right away. Through tips you would have money every day.

"I had to learn the different foods. The orders were all abbreviated. When food came out of the kitchen I waited for the other waitresses to take their food, and I took what was left and hoped for the best.

"Then I started working at the cash register and that was a fiasco. I thought a nickel had more value than a dime because it's a little bigger. So I messed that up."

"It's just automatic when we grow up with it."

"They were patient, and they trained me."

"What else was hard for you?"

"It was stressful trying to fit in. Even to this day, women thought we took their men away. You see, there was that stigma."

"Well you did, kinda."

They both laugh, further easing tension between them, as humor is wont to do.

"I didn't let that bother me. If they can't keep them here and they go over there and we meet them, so what? That was my attitude."

"So there."

"I had a green card and concentrated on learning enough English to pass my U.S. citizenship exam. My husband got orders for Japan, and I wanted to make sure I could get back into the States.

"Other military wives really helped me. It takes most people five years to make American citizenship, and I did it in 15 months."

"It was that important to you?"

"You can't stand with each foot in different countries. It's almost like having a split personality.

"You choose one or the other. I am only an American citizen, not a German anymore.

"Now I was carrying Bryce's child, Karin. She was born in America. I didn't have a crib, and we couldn't afford one on a military salary.

"I pulled a bottom drawer from our dresser and put Karin in that. She says she's claustrophobic to this day!"

24

My Untold Story—1957

By the time I received and threw away Wayne's letter, I learned I was pregnant for the third time, with his child that I named Tomas.

Bryce's baby was my fourth. Hitler gave a Mother's Cross of Honor for bearing children in honor and support of the German nation. I would have earned a bronze cross for my four. For six children, he gave a silver cross, for eight, a gold cross.

Bryce promised to adopt my other children, giving them his name as my father would have wanted.

When he was transferred back to the States, we accompanied him as a family.

But we left one child behind. Klaus remained fragile with a heart murmur and needed medical treatment we could not afford.

While we were still in Germany, Bryce met a lawyer with the French military. He and his wife wanted a child but couldn't conceive one. As Bryce got to know them better, he persuaded me they would be good adoptive parents who could also afford his medical care.

When Klaus was just three years old, I bought a soft blue rabbit with floppy ears and handed them both to the couple Bryce had chosen for his new home. It was the hardest thing I had ever done.

His adoptive parents were Jewish and raised him in France. When she was a teenager, his adoptive mother was forced onto a bus, maybe even one I saw as it motored through Köln with black curtains over the windows.

But she seized a fleeting opportunity to escape out a door and roll into a ditch without being seen. We were two mothers bound by one son, one a birth mother, the other an adoptive mother, escaping a similar fate as the war ground down.

Years later, pre-internet, I went into a small-town library to search for my son. I had one clue, remembering the last name of his adoptive father and that he was an international attorney. I traced him to an office in New York City, a week before he would close that office.

It was another of the miracles of timing that have defined my life.

Klaus grew up to be an engineer. The next time I saw him was in Paris, then later in Germany, and then when he traveled to the United States to see me and meet his siblings.

Of all my children, Klaus, raised by others after the age of three, is closest to my soul mate.

Small Luxuries

25

New Assignment—1959

"Wait. Wait. Was Sergeant Bryce my great-grandfather?"

Seeming not to hear, Gisela continues.

"After my husband reported to his new assignment on Kyushu Island, I followed with Karin five months later. It was a very long trip.

"Back then you could live very cheap in Japan. I had a maid. Can you believe I had a maid? Only $25 a month. She took care of Karin when she was little. I loved the Japanese people. You didn't go into a store to shop for clothes, you just bought fabric. A seamstress would make it into whatever you wanted, specifically to fit you. Bryce had a sharkskin suit made."

"Sharkskin?"

"Fabric with a twill weave. It's not quite shiny, but with a sheen that makes it look expensive.

"We couldn't afford that luxury stateside, and he was very proud of it. I even got a matching suit with a skirt."

"Did you learn to speak Japanese?"

"I had more chances to practice English because we lived among so many Americans.

"Then I got involved in the NCO club. Another officer's wife, she was from California, and I started bringing entertainers to the club. Singers and small bands on weekends. She had connections from back home. It was so popular we were asked to extend it to other bases."

"Really? That's dope."

"It required some travel to those bases to help set it up, and our husbands said 'no.' Men can stand in your way sometimes.

"But then I decided to return to the States."

"Do you mean alone?"

"Things weren't going well between Bryce and me."

"Good thing you had your citizenship."

26

MY UNTOLD STORY—1963

I moved to Japan with more than Karin, my fourth child. I also traveled with Tomas, who had measles that I hid by pulling a hat over his face, and my first-born, Petra. The long trip with three children, one of them sick, was exhausting for all of us. I fell asleep during a layover in Midway and we nearly missed take-off of a commuter flight to my husband's base.

Petra and Tomas went to an American school. Tomas was outgoing and easily made friends with both American and Japanese children.

One day he was playing with Japanese children, and kids being kids, they decided to pick up rocks and throw them at a passing train.

It was dangerous, of course. The train stopped suddenly, and crew jumped out to run after them.

The incident was immediately reported to Bryce's commander, and he feared he would be demoted. Bryce was a Master Sergeant at the time, and would lose a stripe, pay, and retirement level.

After Tomas came home that day, Bryce beat him with a belt so hard that the buckle broke his sternum. I tried to stop his rage, flashing back to the time my father beat me for not coming home directly after school. *Mutter* tried to stop *Vati* too. We both failed.

Family money was always tight. He drank a lot and often bought drinks for the bar. Sometimes there wasn't enough money left for rent. But the beating was the tipping point, the moment I decided to leave him and go back to the States.

Through Bryce I was a member of the NCO. I went into the club and asked for a map of the States.

I didn't know much about the United States. I'd only seen New York and didn't want to go back there. I asked for a penny, closed my eyes, and tossed it on the map. It landed on Washington State.

I said, "That's where I'm going."

Just before leaving, I had some unfinished business.

I picked up a pair of shears, cut the legs off Bryce's prized sharkskin pants, and put them on the hanger under his suit coat.

Fresh Start

27

On My Own

"Did you go back to New York?"

"After four years in Japan I was ready for someplace new. I'd seen photos of Washington State, the mountains, and the Pacific Coast and thought it would be a beautiful place for a fresh start. I landed at the Seattle airport with three suitcases and $110."

"I guess you couldn't ask him for money when you were leaving him."

"Fortunately, I was still a military wife so we could fly free. I took a taxi to a nearby Mom & Pop motel and asked how far to the nearest army base. Even though I'd passed my citizenship test I was still learning English.

"I was able to make the motel owner understand my situation."

"Did you explain why you were there?"

"I never reveal everything, Jessica."

Jessica nods. Yes, she already knew that.

"The motel owner didn't charge me for the night and then he drove us to Fort Lewis Army Base in his Cadillac.

"I went to the housing rental office and told them I wanted a job at the Officers' Club, and I needed a car. They wanted $100 deposit."

"You had only $110!"

"Then I met a couple who offered to let us stay with them.

"In a short time, I got a job as waitress at the NCO club. The man drove me to work and his wife babysat. I soon made enough to buy an old Dart and rent my own apartment. I wanted to get closer to Seattle."

"Why leave the base? You had a job there."

"I was still married but I knew I needed to separate myself from military life.

"Someone told me about a German restaurant in Seattle looking for help. I told the owners I needed a job and a place to live.

"They were happy to get me, and they had a small house I could rent within walking distance.

"People helped me all along the way. I like to give back whatever I can now, because I have had so much help. I am sure our Heavenly Father was looking out for me. I didn't know it then, but I know it now."

"I'm not religious, Grandma."

"Someday you will look back and see miracles in your own life.

"I loved the Northwest Coast. The air is so fresh. There is nothing like the smell of ocean.

"After a year my mother got seriously ill in Germany. The restaurant owners gave me money to go back, and I stayed with her as she recovered. The Red Cross was able to get my husband out of Japan to stay with the children while I was gone. Because of his drinking I kept my fingers crossed that he would be okay with the kids. But he was."

"The kids? You've only told me about one."

"And then he got orders for Fort Lewis. We all moved back into base housing with him."

"You took him back?"

"What was I thinking? Now Bryce was drinking through all his pay. A year later I divorced him.

"A good friend, another military wife, had a job in the records office at the base hospital. That's how I eventually learned Bryce had cancer. None of us knew that.

"Five years later he took his life in a gas oven."

"A gas oven. How ironic is that. Did you marry again?"

"I still had children at home. A child needs a father."

28

MY UNTOLD STORY

How many husbands did I have? Some were so long ago I cannot remember their names. Like many children of that war, I spiraled through an ongoing cycle of relationships.

There was Mark, a salesman. Paul, a liquor distributor. Larry, a hotel manager. Dan, a building contractor.

All drank too much. They provided the physical intimacy I craved. They were reckless with money, leaving me to ever fend for myself, and nearly destitute at the end.

"Men are all the same, they all piss on you," my mother warned when my father sought a divorce after years of philandering.

Yet in their arms I forever sought the love and acceptance of a distant father.

When I worked as a bartender, one of my many occupations, my seductive Barbie looks ensured charged banter and high tips.

I met several of my husbands in bars. How could I be surprised when they drank up our money?

29

THE CHEST

"Let's have some lunch.

"I thawed quiche from the freezer I can heat in a few minutes. There's no meat."

Gisela makes a salad of chopped celery, topping it with blue cheese curds, almond halves, a drizzle of olive oil, and fresh ground pepper.

They sit in their usual places, Gisela in her recliner, Jessica in a wooden chair next to her, facing the television set.

Gisela turns on the midday news while they finish eating. Jessica would leave early afternoon to drive home, with still unanswered questions.

The local news station, which usually broadcasts the local weather forecast, cuts to their network affiliate with breaking news.

Dozens of men were marching through American streets, blocking traffic while carrying flags with swastikas, raising their right arms in a stiff Nazi salute.

A banner across the bottom of the screen reads, "National Guard Troops Are Standing By."

Jessica and Gisela stare at the screen in silence.

Gisela takes a deep breath. She turns slowly, puts her hand on Jessica's arm and looks directly into her eyes.

"The soldier I met at the dance? I liked him. After so much sadness he made me smile again. I'd never had much alcohol, and one night after a dance I had too much.

"He never knew about the baby. He was transferred back to the States. I didn't know his last name."

"How old were you?"

"Eighteen."

"Was he my great-grandfather?"

"Yes. Yes he was."

"So does my grandmother know anything about her father? Did you ever tell her about him?"

"I said her father was an American, which was true. We didn't talk about the details. No one asked. At least not until you."

"I'm 18. I can't even imagine having a baby for years yet."

Gisela eases out of her chair, reaches for her walker, and heads for a corner of her living room.

She lifts a basket overflowing with skeins of multi-colored yarn, uncovering the blue wooden chest.

"Jessica, come help me."

At Gisela's urging, Jessica opens the lid, leaning it back against the wall. Inside are notebooks, photo albums, loose pages with handwritten notes. An old camera, a Leica.

"These are stories and poems I've written about my life. My untold stories.

"You are free to read as much as you like. You, and the rest of my family."

Gisela feels somehow lighter, the burden of unspoken secrets lifted.

Jessica texts her mother. "I'm going to stay another day. Maybe more."

THE NAZI'S DAUGHTER

A 10-Minute Play

For Book Clubs and Discussion Groups

Bring Gisela's story to life and give it voice. With only two characters, this short play can easily be read or performed for small groups.

The manuscript was one of 10 plays chosen for production in 2025 at Lakeshore Center for the Arts in Westfield, New York, out of more than 200 worldwide submissions. It was voted among audience favorites.

THE NAZI'S DAUGHTER

CAST

GISELA, a woman who grew up in Nazi Germany

JESSICA, her great-granddaughter

SCENE

A contemporary condo with kitchen, dining table and chairs, living room, recliner, television, sliding glass and entrance doors.

GISELA

(Gisela wears jeans and a sweatshirt. Stands and speaks directly to audience.)

I woke up with a smile. It was my 8th birthday and I couldn't wait to share it with Sadie. We walked to school together.

We'd sit for dinner promptly at 6 p.m., my mother and father and little brother and me.

Earlier that day I gave each child in my classroom a piece of chocolate wrapped in shiny blue foil. My parents taught me that when you celebrate a birthday you give treats to others. *Vati*, I started to say. Chocolate was scarce, and I wanted to tell him how excited my classmates were about my gift. But I stopped. Speaking without first being spoken to could mean a slap across the face, even on your birthday.

Two days later, the Royal Air Force began raining bombs on Köln, our hometown.

(She shifts slightly, transitioning to the present.)

One day in mid-December, I found a hand-addressed card in my mailbox. It was from my great-granddaughter Jessica.

"Dear Grandma,

Can I come visit you between Christmas and New Years?

Love, Jessica."

I turned the card over to see if more was written on the back. There wasn't. Why did Jessica want to come? My grandchildren and great-grandchildren barely know me, and I know little of their lives. Even my own children feel distant.

Black-out

Loud knock on the door. Jessica enters, wearing jeans, a puffer jacket and wool knit hat, and giant wrap-around sunglasses. Red, white and green stripes of the Italian flag are knit into her long neck scarf.

JESSICA

Hi, Grandma!

(Jessica turns around)

How do you like my Italian vibe?

GISELA

You look expensive.

Come, take off your coat and sit. I made a traditional German lunch. We have assorted cheeses, three kinds of sausage, mustards and breads.

JESSICA

Oh, I should have told you before I came. I'm vegetarian. You do know that sausage is filled with poisonous preservatives

GISELA

Ja, ja. But I'm still here.

JESSICA

Grandma, I have exciting news. I'm applying to be an exchange student in Germany.

GISELA

Ja? Germany? Not Italy?

JESSICA

I already know my Italian side from my dad. I don't know anything about the half of me that's German. I want to hear about life in Germany.

GISELA

You mean my life? That's in the past. There's nothing to say.

JESSICA

Grandma. What about your family?

GISELA

My mother and dad and little brother and I lived in an apartment. Every night after dinner *Vati* wound his prized silver pocket watch. Our meals ran by his watch. *Frühstück*, 7 a.m. *Mittagessen*, noon. *Abendessen*, 6 p.m.

JESSICA

I know those words. Breakfast, lunch, and dinner. Did you go to school?

GISELA

Of course. I'd pass Sadie's apartment in the next block and we'd walk to school together. She was my best friend.

JESSICA

What did your dad do?

GISELA

He worked for the government.

(Stands up and addresses audience. Jessica nibbles food, oblivious to what Gisela is saying.)

I know he was a Nazi, but I can't make myself say the word. One night I woke up when he came home late. From a crack in my bedroom door I could see his pants were torn and bloodied, and he was wearing a saber. Later, that night was called *Kristallnacht*.

A few days earlier, our teacher had called Sadie and me to the front of the class. She asked other students to look at us and compare our eyes and nose and hair to pictures in a book.

"Which one is the Aryan?" she asked. "They are a special race who will carry Germany 1,000 years into the future." We returned to our seats in silence.

Every year my dad took his pocket watch to Heinen, a master watch repairer, for cleaning. This year he put it in a kitchen drawer and never talked about having it cleaned by him again.

Vati said "Shop closed. The monkey is sick."

(Gisela returns to table and faces Jessica.)

JESSICA

Grandma, were you alive during the war?

GISELA

Ja, ja I was.

JESSICA

How scary was that?

GISELA

We went on living. After the bombing started we'd listen for air raid sirens and run down to the coal cellar for shelter. One night we had fresh snow, followed by clear skies and a full moon.

It was bright as day. Bombs fell so close that we could hear them buzzing in our shelter before they exploded.

JESSICA

Oh my god!

(She absently crosses herself)

GISELA

(To audience. She speaks in a dispassionate way that sounds like it happened to someone else.)

Everything went black. Outside, there were flames everywhere. We could smell burning flesh. Our apartment windows were broken and our stuff had all flown out. The next morning I learned that Sadie's apartment building was destroyed. My best friend was dead.

(To Jessica)

After it was over we barely spoke of that night. What good would it do? It was time to move on.

JESSICA

Just move on?!

GISELA

The trains were still running and my mom and brother and I left the city. My dad stayed behind to work. A half-day later we reached a small village.

A farm family let us stay in a house on their land. It was just a shack, with a couple of rooms. We used an outhouse. The only running water in the house was a faucet. That was our kitchen. There was a wood stove for heat and cooking.

JESSICA

It sounds like summer camp. How long did you stay there?

GISELA

Several years.

JESSICA

Several years?!

GISELA

There was nowhere to move. One day *Mutter* was summoned to report to the next village with me and my brother. She said "We're not going."

The next morning she threw dry branches and newspapers in a burn barrel, lit a match, and told me to bring down our personal documents. She added them to the fire, along with our copy of *Mein Kampf.*

JESSICA

You had a copy of *Mein Kampf?*

GISELA

Every German household had one. A few weeks later, the wireless broadcast "Our *Führer*, Adolf Hitler, has fallen." The war was over.

(To audience)

The next day my mother told me she was half Jewish. Even my father did not know. Her refusal to answer that summons, and American liberators, saved our lives.

JESSICA

What did people say after the war ended?

GISELA

Nobody talked about it. We stayed on in the village.

One afternoon, when I was 16, I decided to go to a dance at a beer hall. Frank Sinatra's *Always* was playing on a jukebox and the air was solid with cigarette smoke and the smell of beer. It was filled with American soldiers.

JESSICA

Did anyone ask you to dance?

GISELA

I barely knew how to dance, but one soldier taught me a few steps and we tried to speak a few words. He had a warm smile and we laughed together.

JESSICA

So did you see him again?

GISELA

Ja. We went to another dance. Even though I didn't know English, I could tell he was talking about America.

(Gisela stands up and addresses audience. Jessica scrolls through her cell phone, unaware of what Gisela is saying.)

It was just a dance.

Some people would call me a slut, and maybe I was. I happily melted into the warm arms of the American GI who had smiled back, leaning my face close to his.

We went dancing a second time. After we left the hall and I'd already had some beers, he poured me a glass of vodka from a bottle in his car. Soon everything went hazy. I vaguely remember following him into a wooded area nearby.

My dance partner was transferred shortly, never knowing he had fathered Petra, my first child, Jessica's grandmother.

(Gisela returns to Jessica.)

JESSICA

What happened with the guy you met at the dance?

GISELA

He was transferred back to the States.

JESSICA

Then what?

GISELA

I found a job with a doctor and his wife in a bigger town. I stayed in their home week nights and went home on weekends. I had to walk two and one-half hours each way.

JESSICA

I can't believe how far you walked.

GISELA

There was no public transportation. I worked so we'd have money to live on.

(Gisela gets up and again addresses audience. Jessica returns to cell phone.)

I was walking home late one afternoon when a Jeep with two American soldiers slowed. One asked if I'd like a ride. I was tired and climbed gratefully into the back. When the driver turned onto a narrow wooded trail I knew I'd made a huge mistake. The soldier who offered me a ride raped me in the back seat while the driver watched. Then he pushed me out of the car. After I was sure they'd left, I hurried home and didn't tell anyone.

Nine months later I gave birth to a son. He was gravely ill and we took him to a hospital that was still short staffed. On one of my visits, I could tell no one was looking after Klaus. I was sure he would die there, so I unhooked needles and tubes, grabbed him and strode out the front door.

My mother nursed him back to health and cared for Petra while I looked for another job.

(Gisela resumes conversation with Jessica.)

JESSICA

Couldn't you find work closer to home?

GISELA

Yes. I also met Wayne. We were engaged for three years when he was transferred Stateside. He gave me some money and told me to come to the States later.

JESSICA

How much later did you come?

GISELA

I got a letter from him in English that I couldn't read, so I threw it away. I never heard from him again.

(Gisela addresses audience. Jessica returns to cell phone.)

By the time I received Wayne's letter and threw it away, I'd learned I was pregnant with his child that I named Tomas.

(To Jessica.)

Before long I met Bryce, a master sergeant. He reminded me of my father. My mother and little brother both liked him.

JESSICA

You finally met a guy who stayed around?

GISELA

Bryce and I were married in our village, and we came to the United States on a troop carrier. Soon after we arrived, I learned I was pregnant with our daughter.

JESSICA

Wait. Was Sergeant Bryce my great-grandfather?

GISELA

(Gisela addresses the audience. Jessica returns to phone and does not hear her.)

Bryce promised to adopt my other children. When he was transferred back to the States, we accompanied him as a family. But Klaus was left behind. We couldn't afford his medical care, and Bryce had met a lawyer who wanted to adopt a child with his wife. He convinced me they would be good parents who could also pay for care.

When Klaus was just three, I bought a soft blue rabbit with floppy ears and handed them both to the couple. It was the hardest thing I had ever done.

His adoptive parents were Jewish. As a teenager his adoptive mother was forced onto a bus headed for a concentration camp, but she was able to escape out a door undetected. We were two mothers bound by one son, escaping a similar fate as the war ground down.

(Gisela returns to table & Jessica.)

Later my husband was re-assigned to Japan. I followed with our daughter five months later. But after a year I decided to return to the States.

JESSICA

By yourself?

GISELA

Things weren't going well between Bryce and me.

JESSICA

Was he my great grandfather?

GISELA

(Addresses audience.)

Tomas was playing with Japanese kids when they all started throwing rocks at passing trains. When he came home, my husband beat him with a belt so hard that the buckle broke his sternum.

I decided right then to leave him and go back to the States.

(Returns to Jessica.)

JESSICA

You won't tell me about my great-grandfather. I still know almost nothing about your life in Germany. I may as well drive home tonight instead of staying over like I'd planned.

GISELA

(GISELA stops, looking Jessica directly in the eye.)

Jessica, the soldier I met at the dance? I liked him. After so much sadness he made me smile again. I'd never had alcohol, and one night after a dance he poured me too much.

He never knew about the baby. He was transferred back to the States. I didn't know his last name.

JESSICA

Was he my great-grandfather?

GISELA

Ja, ja, he was.

JESSICA

So does my grandmother know about her father? Did you ever tell her?

GISELA

I said her father was an American, which was true. No one asked about details. Not until you. Jessica, I see something of myself in you. You deserve to know the truth about all my children, and their fathers.

Let's get a good night's rest and I'll tell you about them in the morning.

(Jessica turns and silently exits to bedroom).

(Gisela turns on cable television and reads banner across the bottom.)

"Men marched through American streets today carrying flags with swastikas, raising their arms in the Nazi salute."

(Gisela closes her eyes, drops her head into her hands and sighs.)

CURTAIN

Judy Shuler grew up in a German community in rural Wisconsin. She currently lives in rural Western New York.

More about the author and her other books can be found at *wordsalwaysmatter.wordpress.com*

9 7 9 8 2 1 8 8 4 8 0 4 0